Speck

By

Dave and Pat Sargent

Illustrated by
Jane Lenoir

Ozark Publishing, Inc.
P.O. Box 228
Prairie Grove, AR 72753

Sargent, Dave, 1941-
    Speck / by Dave and Pat Sargent ; illustrated by Jane
Lenoir. — Prairie Grove, AR : Ozark Publishing, ©2001.
    ix, 36 p. : col. ill. ; 23 cm.   (Saddle-up series)

    "Good Attitude"—Cover.
    SUMMARY: A black patterned leopard horse is proud
when his lady boss, Betsy Ross, is selected as seamstress for
the United States flag, and he makes a special effort to take
care of her. Includes factual information on leopard horses.
    ISBN: 1-56763-663-2   (hc)
           1-56763-664-0 (pbk)

    1. Ross, Betsy, 1752-1836—Juvenile fiction. [1. Ross,
Betsy, 1752-1836—Fiction. 2. Horses—Fiction. 3. Flags—
United States—Fiction. 4. Robbers and outlaws—Fiction.]
I. Sargent, Pat, 1936- II. Lenoir, Jane, 1950-   ill. III. Title.
IV. Series.

    PZ10.3. S243Sn 2001
    [E]—dc21   2001-002607

Printed in the United States of America

Inspired by

a couple of black patterned leopard horses we saw early one morning in a lush green field beside the road. We slowed down to get a closer look, but the road was narrow and there was not a safe place to pull over.

Dedicated to

all kids with freckles. We had a few
freckles when we were young.

Foreword

Speck is a horse with a good attitude. He loves life and his job. His lady boss is Betsy Ross. Now, tell us. Do you know that name?

When three bad men try to rob Speck's lady boss, he quickly goes into action. When one of the men grabs the end of a bolt (roll) of pretty material, Speck grabs the bolt of material and takes off! He runs around and around the bad men and wraps them up tight. That's when his friend, Grey, shows up with the sheriff.

Now, back to Speck's lady boss, Betsy Ross. What did she do? Okay. We'll give you a clue. It has something to do with the three colors *red*, *white*, and *blue*.

Contents

Speck

If you would like to have the authors of the Saddle Up Series visit your school, free of charge, call 1-800-321-5671 or 1-800-960-3876.

One

Lady Boss Betsy Ross

The entire city of Philadelphia was bustling with activity. Horses hitched to wagons and buggies were moving along the narrow dirt streets. Speck the black patterned leopard smiled and spoke to the horses as he proudly trotted passed them.

"Good morning, Sorrel!" he nickered. "Isn't it a beautiful day?"

"Yes, it is," the sorrel replied. "But it's a shame that we have to work today. The way I see it, you and I should be munching on grassy goodies and running through a lush green pasture."

"That sounds fine, Sorrel," Speck agreed with a chuckle, "but it's important that I take my lady boss Betsy Ross to the upholstery shop today. She has a lot of work to do, and her work keeps me supplied with plenty of oats."

"Hmmm," the sorrel mumbled. "I guess you're right. I better stop complaining about my boss and his work schedule."

The black patterned leopard nodded his head and trotted on down the street toward the shop. A small group of ladies was standing in front of the door when he and Lady Boss stopped near the hitching post.

"Hello, ladies," Betsy Ross said as she climbed out of the buggy. "I'll hurry. I'll be open for business in a few minutes."

"We aren't here to purchase anything, Betsy," a lady responded. "We just want to congratulate you."

"Congratulate me?" Betsy said in a shocked voice. "For what?"

Hmmm, Speck thought. It sounds like these women have heard something that we don't know about. Wonder what it is?

"Shame on you, Betsy Ross!" one of the ladies exclaimed. "Aren't you excited about the news?"

"What news?" Lady Boss Betsy asked with a bewildered expression on her face.

The group of women smiled and looked at one another.

One of the ladies said, "Well, last night my husband said that the Philadelphia Navy Board has chosen you to make the ships' colors."

Betsy Ross raised her eyebrows and asked, "Make the ships' colors? I don't understand."

"Neither do I," Speck agreed quietly. "But it sounds exciting."

Once again the group of ladies giggled. Finally a rather large lady stepped forward and put her hand on Betsy's shoulder.

"My dear," she said in a husky tone of voice, "it means that the navy wants to commission you to make the flags for their ships'."

"Oh!" Betsy Ross squealed. "That would be wonderful! Since my husband passed away, business has been a bit slow."

The black patterned leopard nodded his head in agreement.

"Lady Boss is trying real hard to succeed as a seamstress. She will certainly do the navy a good job on those ships' colors." Speck smiled as he added, "Now that she knows what ships' colors are."

Moments later, Betsy entered the shop. Speck watched her put the OPEN sign in the window. He was happy to see her smiling as she arranged the upholstery fabrics along the countertops for the customers to see.

The black patterned leopard saw the man from the livery stable approaching, and he nickered a friendly greeting.

"Are you about ready to go to the stable for the day, Speck?" the man asked.

Speck nodded his head before nuzzling the fellow's cheek.

"I like you," he murmured.

"You are both kind and good to me."

The man tapped on the window of the shop and waved to Betsy Ross before climbing into the buggy. And a moment later, Speck was trotting up the street to the livery stable.

"I really don't mind waiting for Lady Boss to close her shop," Speck muttered with a smile, "especially since this livery stable man gives me a couple of treats during the day. He's a good friend!"

The late afternoon sun felt hot to Speck as he and the livery stable man returned to the upholstery shop.

"It's about closing time for your Betsy Ross," the man said as he tied Speck to the hitching post.

Once again he tapped on the window and waved to Lady Betsy. Then he retrieved another lump of sugar from his shirt pocket and held it out to Speck.

The black patterned leopard nickered appreciatively before he took the sugar and began munching on it.

"I'll see you tomorrow, Speck," the man said with a wave of his hand. A moment later, Speck watched him disappear among the men and women who were walking on the boardwalk in front of the stores.

The black patterned leopard was standing quietly when three gentlemen stopped at the door of the upholstery shop. They were talking excitedly among themselves.

"This is the upholstery shop that is owned by Mrs. Betsy Ross, gentlemen," the tall fellow said. "Shall we go in and see if she will accept our offer?"

Without further hesitation, they entered the shop and closed the door behind them. Well, Speck thought. Maybe they're from the Navy Board. I hope so. It would make Lady Boss very happy. Forty-five minutes later, the men left the shop, and Speck noticed that Lady Boss was indeed happy. She shook the hand of the tall man and then thanked each one.

"It looks like she got the job!" Speck shouted.

All the other horses traveling down the street congratulated Speck and his lady boss as they passed.

"You'll get extra oats tonight," Black said with a chuckle.

"I sure wish my boss would get some good news," the dun muttered. "He's been about as cranky as an old grizzly bear the last few days."

"My boss gives me a bite of hard candy when times are good," the piebald said with a smile.

"Thanks, friends," Speck said. "I'll see you all tomorrow."

As Betsy Ross stepped onto the boardwalk in front of him, he pawed the ground with his front hoof in greeting. He thought cheerfully, tomorrow should be one fine day!

13

Two

Flags For The Ships

The next several weeks in the year of 1776 were very busy. Speck took Betsy Ross to the upholstery shop each day. Then he patiently waited at the livery stable while she sewed ships' colors into flags for the Philadelphia Naval Board. Every evening she climbed into the buggy with a tired but happy expression on her face. Speck really admired her.

The sun was low on the western horizon one Friday evening when the black patterned leopard horse and his lady boss started moving slowly toward home.

"You need a break from work for a while, Lady Boss," Speck said. "I think you need to take the long way home and enjoy the country-side."

Betsy snapped the reins on his rump and tried to turn him toward home. But Speck calmly continued to walk straight down the road.

"Speck!" she shouted. "What are you doing?"

"I'm going to take you for a quiet buggy ride in the country," he said, "whether you want it or not."

Betsy tried to turn the horse around several times, but he ignored the commands. Soon they were out of the city and winding their way through the peaceful countryside.

The twilight of day was calm and cool. Speck knew that Betsy was enjoying the buggy ride as she leaned back and softly hummed a familiar melody.

"Ah," he murmured, "this is what she needs. A chance to relax. I wish we could do this every day."

An hour later, Speck trotted up the lane toward home. He felt good when Lady Boss Betsy stepped from the buggy. She looked so refreshed and rested.

Betsy Ross gently stroked the black patterned leopard on the neck and said, "Thank you so much, Speck. It seems I do nothing but work anymore."

Speck nuzzled her on the cheek and murmured, "You are welcome, Lady Boss."

The next morning Speck and Betsy went by the railroad station to pick up some bolts of fabric that had been brought in by rail. The man at the station carefully loaded them in the buggy beside Betsy. A moment later, Speck was again trotting up the road.

Suddenly three men stepped in front of Speck, and he came to a halt. He nickered and pawed the ground as they looked at Betsy Ross.

"You're much too pretty to be out traveling by yourself," one of the dirty-looking men said.

"She is not by herself!" Speck growled.

"She looks lonesome to me," another troublemaker added.

"She is not lonesome!" Speck screamed. "I am with her."

"Would you look at all that pretty material!" the third culprit said. "I think I want some of that to make me a shirt."

As the other bad men agreed, Speck suddenly reared up on his hind legs. His front hooves lashed through the air.

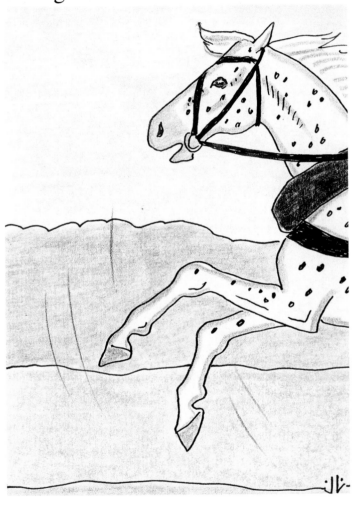

One man grabbed for the bolt of material, and another tried to grab Betsy. The man had one end of the bolt of material in his hand when Speck took off. As he raced around and around in a circle, the material actually wrapped around the three bad men.

After many loops, Speck finally stopped circling. Betsy Ross jumped out of the buggy and, with the black patterned leopard standing guard, tied the three bundled men to a tree. They had just finished when Speck heard a friend approaching.

"What's the trouble here?" the grey horse asked.

"Whew," Speck replied. "I'm sure glad you brought the sheriff. These three bad men were trying to rob and hurt Lady Boss."

"Take Lady Boss to her shop, Speck," the grey said. "And don't worry about these fellows anymore. Sheriff and I will take care of them!"

"Thanks, Grey. You're a good friend," Speck yelled as he once again trotted up the street toward the upholstery shop of Betsy Ross.

"My job is much bigger than just pulling a buggy," he muttered. "My job is more important than just getting Lady Boss to work on time. I am her friend, her transportation, and her guard horse, too."

Three

The Stars and Stripes Flag

One week later, a messenger was waiting for Lady Boss as Speck stopped in front of the upholstery shop. As Betsy unlocked the front door, the man smiled and bowed before handing her an important-looking piece of paper.

"A committee has met," the man said, "to choose the seamstress who will make the Stars and Stripes flag for the United States, Mrs. Ross. And it appears that you were the chosen one."

Speck felt his heart beating fast with pride and excitement. Wow! he thought. This is a great honor for my lady boss.

"Are . . . are you sure," Betsy stuttered, "that you have the right Betsy Ross?"

The messenger smiled and then nodded his head. "Yes," he said. "You are the chosen one. I've brought you a sketch that shows what the committee has in mind."

Speck looked it over good.

"The committee?" Betsy said. "Who is on the committee?"

The messenger smiled and said, "George Washington, Robert Morris, and George Ross. The three men feel very comfortable, Mrs. Ross, in their decision to offer you the job of seamstress."

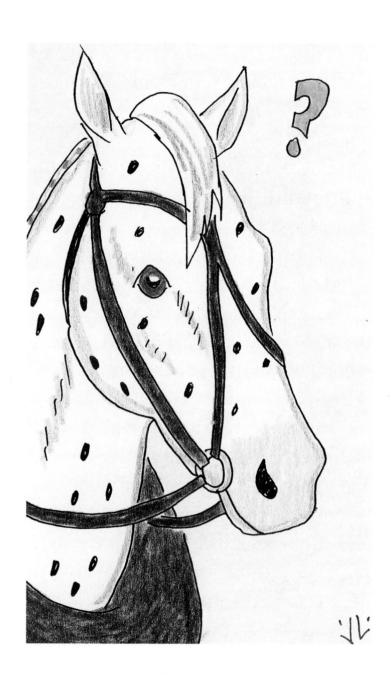

"This is wonderful!" Speck shouted. "This is a great honor for Lady Boss, and I know that she will do a fine job."

That evening, as the CLOSED sign was placed in the window of the upholstery shop, Betsy Ross looked at Speck and smiled. Minutes later, the black patterned leopard was proudly trotting through the streets of Philadelphia on his way to the Ross home. Suddenly he felt the reins on his rump, commanding him to turn from the house.

"This is not Friday evening," he said. "We always go for a ride in the country on Friday evenings."

"This is a very special day, Speck," Betsy Ross said. "I want to celebrate it with you by taking a quiet buggy ride in the country."

Speck perked up right away as he happily changed directions.

He thought, Mrs. Betsy Ross is going to sew a flag with thirteen red and white stripes and thirteen stars on a field of blue. And then she will live forever in American history.

Speck walked on for several minutes with good thoughts rushing through his head. I just wonder if anybody will remember a certain black patterned leopard horse who took good care of Mrs. Betsy Ross. Oh well, it doesn't really matter. Life is good and just getting better and better!

Four

Black Patterned Leopard Facts

The description *leopard* is used for horses that are all white with spots, or that have blankets, with colored spots on the white. These colored spots may be from a few centimeters to several centimeters across.

In some *patterned leopards* the spots seem-to flow out of the flank and over the body of the horse.

In the *unpatterned leopard* the spots are usually rounder and do not appear to flow out of the flank.

A *black patterned leopard* may make you think it is an *Appaloosa.* except that it has a thick mane and tail, which is characteristic of the *Noriker* horse. An *Appaloosa* has a very thin mane and tail.

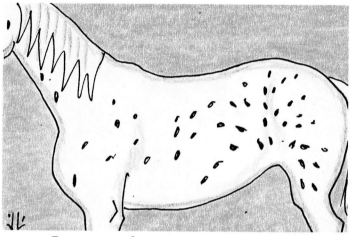

Leopard spots may occur on horses without white bodies, such as the *palomino*, but this is not very common. Dark spots, which may look a little like leopard spots, are sometimes seen on *sorrel*, *chestnut*, and *palomino* horses.